SIDE BY SIDE

Short stories and Poems

John Gumbs

Published by John Gumbs
Publishing partner: Paragon Publishing, Rothersthorpe
First published 2021
© John Gumbs 2021, London

ISBN 978-1-78222-845-5

Book design, layout and production management by Into Print
www. intoprint.net
+44 (0)1604 832149

CONTENTS

CHAPTERS

POEMS

POEMS CONTINUED

SHORT STORY

1.

CHANGING TO LIGHT

Heidi and I were discussing the trip to Andromeda. That in itself is going to be some trip, at least we have some help from the space people. And the disc that they gave us has quite a lot of instructions.

Heidi said, "We have to have a very good ship to get us there."

I said, "I think it is possible. We can do it. First, we must check everything out properly."

"It is a *very* long way," Heidi said, "over 2,500 million light years."

"Wait a minute," I said to her. "That's pretty far. How are we going to get a ship to travel that distance?"

"We just have to look at some ships on the disc. Most of them change to light," Heidi said.

"Meaning?"

"Capable of travelling at the speed of light which is about 299,792 kilometers per second." She said.

"How foolish we are, talking about a ship to take us there. We're forgetting that the space people taught us how to travel without a ship." I said.

Heidi said, "We haven't forgotten how to do it, have we?"

"You were the first one who learned it from them. We just have to concentrate on where we want to be."

"Give me your hand," Heidi said, "and let's concentrate on a certain place, and go there."

We concentrated hard, and found ourselves at the place we had concentrated on.

"The power is still there," I said. "We can prepare to go to space anytime we want to!"

"This Andromeda Galaxy is only about 2.5 million light years away. For us that's no problem. We will be there, just like that!" Heidi said.

"There are quite a lot of galaxies in that area. And our own Milky Way is nearest to it. We need to find a sun with planets around it. That would be great!"

Heid said, "We would get to see that black hole, and all those old dying red stars, along with the blue young ones.

"This could be the trip of a lifetime, and we're not travelling in a ship."

"We'll have a lot to tell when we return." Heidi told me. "Our concentration should take us to a planet that can give life, so that when we change back, there'll be no problem. There are so many suns in that area, hope we get to the right one!"

"One that is habitable," I said. "Just like here on Earth."

We were ready now to depart, we held hands, concentrated on a habitable planet in the Andromeda Galaxy, and in no time, we were there standing on the ground. This planet was much bigger than our own Earth, and its revolution around its star was quick. We stayed around for a while, then we concentrated on a black hole. There were many around, and our concentration brought us to one that was really massive. We weren't in the physical, yet we could still experience the greatness and depth of this black hole. After that, we return back to our Earth.

I said to Heidi later on, "Wasn't that *awesome?* An experience that we cannot explain to anyone who is not open to such things."

"You're right! It was way out of the ordinary. Shows you how mysterious life is," she answered.

I said to her, "I've got this idea that we should go back in time to when Jesus was around."

"Can we do that?" she asked, looking surprised. "I mean then, *how* can we do that? Go back in time. The space people didn't teach us that!"

"I know that they didn't tell us about it. But that doesn't mean we shouldn't try. Let's consult the disc and see what it says," I told her.

The disc had information about how to do that. We had to concentrate on the day, the month, the year, the time and the place, then we would find ourselves there. We'll do a few practices first, just to make sure that it works."

Heid said, "It's like programming a computer. What if something goes wrong?"

I said to her, "Our brain is a very complex thing, it takes in all the information that we give it. And with our ability to change to the spiritual side, we just get where we want to forward or backward. You have just experienced what we did when we went to Andromeda."

We studied information that was on the disc about travelling back in time. Making sure we understood the whole procedure, we were now ready to go back in time to Nazareth, Galilee, in the land of Israel … and we were there in no time.

*

The year is 5 BC, the month is October. People were sitting around, old men with a sort of head turban, and long sort of dress with wide sleeves.

In the middle of this place, there was a sort of brick masonry with wooden stuff around. There was a woman there, also in a long dress and sandals on her feet. She was there at a well, and was trying to pull up water.

She saw us still in our modern clothes, the old men around just stared. She said to us, "Who are you? Where did you come from?"

"Okay! Mary," I said. "I will tell you who we are, but don't be afraid."

In surprise she said, "How do you know my name?"

Heidi said, "Your name is known everywhere. Everyone talks about you. And of course, your son Jesus."

"Let me help you draw up this water," I said to her. Of course, your son is still a child, but we already know what he's going to do."

After I had drawn the water, Mary said, "Come with me, sit down, refresh yourselves, and tell me more." She took us to her home with the jar of water across her shoulder.

The house she took us to had a flat roof and what

looks like straw on top. There were wooden blocks on top of bricks on both ends. From the outside, it didn't look much, but when we got inside, it was large and it was clean. There was a lot of pottery around: jars and bowls and cups. This village we found was rather small. There was a small courtyard. We sat around a wooden table with all sort of things to eat which were fruits. We received from her some clay cups and we could have wine diluted with water. She broke a piece of round cake, and gave us both a piece.

2.

THE BABE JESUS

Mary brought the babe Jesus out, and Heidi immediately took him in her arms, then I did the same. Heidi said, "He's a beautiful child, he's going to be tall."

I said, "His hair is black and woolly. He will become a great man in Israel."

Mary said, "We took him to the temple, and a man named Simeon told us many things that we could not understand. Are you messengers from heaven?"

"No, we're not from heaven," Heidi told Mary. "We come from the West, but also from the future." Mary looked baffled. Of course, for a peasant woman, such things would be hard to comprehend. Mary had a beautiful charming face. She was tall and very friendly.

I was surprised when Mary asked, "How is that possible? The future for me is tomorrow., it hasn't arrived yet."

Heidi said, "Mary, where we came from it is the year 2020. You are now living in the Old Time of year 5. Then it means that there are five more years of the Old World, then the New World will start."

"Is that why the prophets were saying, *'At the end of time'*?"

"Yes," I said, "they knew that the end was near."

Heidi said, "Where we come from everything is already known about your son. He became a 'Teacher' and a preacher, and started saying the 'Kingdom is close at hand.'

"Do you know what he means by that?" Mary asked.

"Our scholars who study your bible, the *Torah* and also *The New Testament* which came about because of your son, are still trying to work out many things that have been said," I told her.

"My! This little child has done that?" Mary had the child in her arms, and was looking deep into his face. The child was fast asleep.

"We know quite a lot about your son, Jesus," Heidi said.

"Jesus?" Mary inquired. "My son's name is Yeshua. Joseph is his father."

"In our world," I told her, "they have a different story. Some people don't believe that he existed, others say it's just a myth. They know him as Jesus."

"You have now seen for yourself that it is true. He's just a child, but as you say, he will become great," Mary told us.

Heidi said to Mary softly, "Is it possible to tell us about your own childhood? How you were brought up; and of course, a little about your husband."

Mary said, "My father Joachim was a shepherd, and he married my mother Anna. They lived together for a long time without having any children. They prayed to God, and saying that if they should get a child, they would give it to the temple. My mother found herself pregnant not long afterwards, and I was born to them in the ninth month, around the 8th day of that month, the same year that Herod the Great started to build on the temple."

I said, "We've read that it was the year 19 BC when Herod started on the temple. It wasn't finished until in the New World of 64 AD. The Romans destroyed it in 70 AD."

Heidi said, "I heard too, that it was a beautiful structure. It became the seventh wonder of the Ancient world."

Mary carried on, "It was truly magnificent. The vast structure, the temple complex, separated from the outer court which was the court of the Gentiles. Gentiles weren't allowed in the temple, only if they were converted."

Heidi asked, "Why did you have to go to the temple so young? Was that the custom?"

Mary told us, "It was just the custom of some parents to consecrate their children to the temple of the Lord."

"How long did you stay there?" I asked her.

"When I got to the age of 12, the priests had to get rid of me, so they did a sort of ritual, getting all the old responsible righteous men to come to the temple; all those who were of the line of David, with their rods. The one with the rod that blossomed, and the dove upon his head, is the one that will take me home. The lot fell to Joseph who already had children of his own. He refused at first, but later had to do according to the custom."

"Here in your culture," Heidi said, "women can get married from around the age of 12 and 13, but in our place, you have to be at least 18."

Mary said, "Joseph had to go away quickly to Bethlehem, and I was left in the house. When he came back, he found that I was six months pregnant. He was not in a good mood. Back in the temple, an angel told me that I would get pregnant. I thought that was strange at first, because I haven't been with a man. Again, when I was at home fetching water, the angel appeared to me, and told me much more."

I asked, "Did the angel have wings?"

"No," Mary said. "He came with a shining light around him, told me his name was Gabriel. That's the angel that is always in the *Presence of God.*"

"Who was the High Priest serving at the temple?" Heidi asked.

"It was Simon," Mary said, "Simon ben Boethus. He finished his high priesthood the year Yeshua was born."

"So it was the angel who gave you the name for your son?" I asked her.

"The angel said, 'You're to give him the name Yeshua'."

Just then a tall sturdy woman came into the courtyard, and Mary introduced her as her sister, and wife of Clopas. She took a seat, still surprised to see us in the outfits we were wearing. Mary tried to explain to her that we came from another part of the Earth, and from another time. Whether she understood that I don't know. She was friendly, and looked a bit like Mary. She started telling Mary something about Clopas and the children. I said to her, "We already know that when Yeshua dies, You, Mary and Mary of Magdala will be standing at his cross and weeping."

"How do you know all that?" Mary Clopas asked.

"We are from the future, and we already know what's going to happen," Heidi butted in.

"What else do you know? Mary asked.

I said, "We know that this babe, Yeshua, is going to bring about a new teaching which is spiritual. He will have many followers."

Mary Clopas said, "You mentioned the cross earlier, are you saying Mary's child is going to be crucified?"

Although Heidi and I already knew the answer, I had to think about how to answer the question. Mary took the babe Jesus inside to rest because he was now fast asleep. She came back and made sure we had enough to eat and drink. I turned to Mary Clopas,

"Yes, that's true."

3.

TAKING MARY AND YESHUA TO THE YEAR 2020

Mary said, "From what you've told me, it sounds like you've come from a place that's very beautiful."

Heidi told her, "It is really beautiful. It would be hard to explain it all to you."

"You sure, it's not heaven you came from? And that you're really angels?"

"Not quite Mary," I told her. "Later on, you'll see for yourself."

Heidi told me something that was really interesting. She suggested that we should take Mary and the babe Jesus back with us to stay at least a week. I turned to Mary and said, "We're taking you back with us for a week, along with the babe Yeshua."

"Can you do that? How is that possible?" Mary asked, looking shocked.

Mary Clopas was also amazed, and shocked. "Where are you taking our Mary?" she asked. "Joseph is in Bethlehem, and returning soon."

"She'll be back before he comes home," Heidi said.

"We are taking Mary back," I said, "to see how the future people are living. Don't worry, she'll be safe."

After spending a little more time with Mary, and the

babe Yeshua, and Mary of Clopas, we got Mary inside our circle of hands, she holding Yeshua safely in her arms. Then we just disappeared.

*

We found ourselves in our own country because we had concentrated on that, according to the instructions from the space disc. Light was the cause of everything that we were doing. It is really a complicated tricky business, it could go wrong, if we fail to keep to the instructions.

Mary was still in shock, couldn't believe what had really happened. She was in the year 2020. Her child Yeshua, who almost everyone was following was only a child, just born. Mary saw how different everything was compared to where she came from. She looked around everywhere, astonished. She made comments on all that she saw. She looked at the tall lamp posts hanging over the street. We told her that they are lights in the night.

In the flat we took her to, she saw how everything was laid out, didn't have to go to the well to fetch water. Mary stood there staring at the bookshelves. She was looking at one of the books with the title *Mary, Mother of Jesus*. This was in big letters.

Heidi was intrigued even back in Nazareth to find that Mary was so good with English; she thought Mary could only understand Aramaic and Hebrew, but she understood when we had spoken to her.

Mary was very intelligent. She learned quite a lot when she was in the temple. And most of all, she knew her bible well. Still looking at the bookcase, she went closer, and took out a book entitled *Mary Magdalene*.

"This is Mary of Magdala," she said to us. "She's a child that is born just before I had my son."

"You'll get to know more about her from reading these books," I said. "In fact, there's quite a lot that's going to take place."

In the shed belonging to the flat, Heidi found a pram, it was still looking brand new. She brought it, and Yeshua was placed in it. We asked Mary how she felt being now in the year 2020 compared to where she was from. She told us the feeling was extraordinary. And words had failed her trying to describe it.

Heidi and Mary sat down, and I went and made some soft drinks, explaining as I came back that we have quite a number of drinks around. Then I told Mary, "We shall take you out tomorrow to a Jewish dress shop, and there you can find something for yourself and Yeshua. And one other thing too, the men here are very susceptible to women, and you being so pretty, they'll try and make contact with you. We mustn't let anyone know about who you and the child are. This has to be kept a secret."

Once we were all settled and relaxed, Heidi said to Mary, "Back in Nazareth, you were telling us about the angel who came to you, and about Joseph going away to Bethlehem, and coming back and finding you pregnant!"

Mary said, "The angel said to me that we must call the child Yeshua. He will be called the Son of the Most High and will be great."

"What were you thinking at that moment?" I asked.

"I was lost for words, because I've never been with a man, and I was wondering how could such a thing be possible. But the angel told me that it is all up to God.

17

My parents had angels talk to them before I was born."

"I read in your custom that it is a good thing to have children," I said.

"You'll be a laughing stock if you don't produce a seed," Mary said.

"In one of the books here," I said to her, "your son is talking about the Kingdom of God. He said, if we do not act like little children, we shall not enter it."

4.

SHOWING MARY AROUND

"What is the kingdom of God?" Mary asked.

"Your son said that it is in every one of us," I told her.

"This is all strange to me," she said, "to hear from you that my son will later become a World Religious Teacher."

"That is so as years go by. Is it true that you're from a Royal House?" I asked.

"My father is from the house of Judah, so I'm from that same house, and I'm also from the house of Levi."

"That's the priestly line, isn't it?"

"Yes," she answered. "Goes right back to Aaron, the first priest."

Heidi said, "So your son Yeshua is from both houses?"

"That's correct!"

Some drinks were made, and we offered a glass of orange to Mary.

"Here, in our world," I told her, "we have all sorts of drinks. I know that back at your place it's mainly wine diluted with water.

Mary tasted the drink, and she liked it.

On her way to the flat, she had seen how the houses were arranged with the gardens in the front. It was pleasing to her to see that. She was later shown her room where she would stay. In her heart she was very happy, and told us so. There was a cot in the room as well.

I said to Mary, "Arriving at your place Nazareth, we saw that it was high on a hill."

"That's right, lying to the North. I used to live in Sepphoris, but we moved and came to this village of Nazareth before Sepphoris was destroyed. There are lots of writings about this place Nazareth. Some think it never existed. There were only about twenty families living there at the time."

"I'm now beginning to see," I said to her, "how important Yeshua your son is. He claimed to be king of the Jews."

"Did he?"

"Yes, that's why the chief priests and scribes and elders were up against him. He declared himself to be the Son of God."

Mary said, "Son of God is the title for kings, priests and prophets."

"We know that," I said, "but Yeshua claiming to be the Son of God really got to the Jews, and a big debate started – they calling him an illegitimate child, and he calling them, children of their father."

"That's how our people debate. Question against question; calling names; and finally, picking up stones. My son is not illegitimate!"

Heidi said, "We shall show you some big buildings that are dedicated to your son."

We managed somehow to take Mary out without being recognized. She was from another time, so no one would have been looking out for her. She saw some big cities and their rail and bus systems. Nothing like that was around where she came from.

Mary was really still young, it was her tallness that made her look like a woman. Our lecture about what she was now going to experience gave her a shock, but she wanted to see for herself.

The church we took her to was mainly black, with a few white couples around. We got to the door, and Mary noticed how friendly everyone was.

We were now standing ready to sing the first hymn. After that we sat down.

The preacher started out:

"Our Jesus, is the best. He was pure, without sin, with no deception within him. He is our Saviour. We get to God the Father through him. He is the only man to conquer the world, and to defeat death. He came to show us the way. Only he alone is the light of the world."

Mary had never heard these things before. With her teaching from the temple: it was about the one God – the God of Israel – who is the God of all the nations. On her scroll parchments of the Torah, she knew about Moses and Aaron and Miriam. It was Joshua who took over from Moses, and led the Israelites across the Jordan. She knew all the stories in her bible. But when we told her about the New Testament, it was something she had never heard of.

I said to her, "It is through your son Yeshua, that this New Testament came about."

The preacher started reading from *Isaiah, Chapter 7*. In the temple, when Mary was growing up, she had read Isaiah, and she knew what it was all about. But the preacher had his own interpretation.

Then the time came when people had to go up and confess their sins. Mary was surprised to see so many people in the queue. And was even more surprised when the preacher gave each one a slap on the forehead, sending them backwards into the arms of helpers. After the service had ended, we ask Mary how she felt about it. The singing and the music she enjoyed. She said it was far different from their synagogue service, and also the temple service. We agreed with her.

Coming out the door, the woman sat there said, "What a nice beautiful child you have. Did you enjoy the service?"

Mary answered, "Yes, very much."

*

We found a cafe, went in, had some tea and scones. Mary loved the scones. I said to her, "The church you have just been to, is only one of hundreds all around. Each with its own different style of worshipping, and it's *your* child, they're worshipping."

"He must have done something really great!"

Heidi said, "He did! He came back from the dead, resurrected. The command was given to him from the Father, to lay down his life, and take it up again."

"Rememeber," I said to Mary, "we showed you some buildings where you saw a woman holding a child in her arms; that woman is *you*."

Mary said, "Here, I see lots of statues and images around, but we don't think much of them. And about coming back from the dead, there were much discussions about that where some people believed and others not."

Back inside the flat, Mary told us that she had three sisters and one brother. In our books Many historians were trying to see if they could learn anything about her family. There were so many stories.

I said to Mary, "Soon we are going to take you back, and we'll visit you again in 2050 when in your time, your son Yeshua, is about 30 years old. This is the year he'll start his ministry, and will have been baptised by John the Baptist."

Mary said, "You don't mean John from Elizabeth and Zechariah? He was born before Yeshua, at least six months. I did go and visit Elizabeth. Sone time in March I think it was. John was born around the end of May or June."

Heidi said to Mary, "We don't know if you're going to have more children when you get back. There are quite a lot of children mentioned, and it is not clear to us who they are from."

Mary said, "Joseph had a few children of his own. He is a bit old now. I don't know what's going to happen."

I said, "Maybe you don't have any more children. Yeshua will be the only one."

5.

ARRIVAL AT NAZARETH 27 A.D.

After Mary had seen quite a lot, spoken with many women and men, seen how our society works, we took her back to Nazareth, the village where she lived, then we came back.

*

Heidi and I decided it was time to get back to Nazareth, and visit Mary again. We were now older, but we could still change from matter to spirit or light. We discussed how difficult it was to explain to others what we felt when we changed. As soon as we changed to light, we were no longer in the material form, and within the light, we were just particles. In fact, through the ether, we were magnetic waves travelling in a line of magnetic fields, and those would take us to our destination. Our concentration has to be spot on. This is no time for fooling around. We get to where we want to go just like the instructions tell us.

It was in the year 27 A D that we arrived back in Nazareth just in time to see Mary Cleopas chatting with Mary. She recognized us and saw that we were older, of course they too, were older. Mary had told her of the experience she had with us, and Mary Cleopas could not take it all in. Mary told us that we had just missed

Yeshua; he had gone to the Jordan after he heard that John the Baptist was there and baptizing people for the repentance of sins. I said, "Come on Mary, we'll go out there and see what's going on."

"My son will be surprised to see me there, and you as well!"

Heidi said, "We'll get around that, we'll explain it to him."

It didn't take us long to get to where John the Baptist was baptizing. There were many people there standing beside the water's edge. We came just in time to see Yeshua going down into the water to where the baptist was. The baptist was tall, but not taller than Yeshua. His black hair was uncombed, and his clothes were as if someone had torn them. He had a broad belt around his waist.

Yeshua was in a long white robe with a sort of outer garment. He too, had black hair, crumpled up like wool. His face was sort of longish with deep, penetrating eyes.

There we were at the Jordan River watching Yeshua being baptized by John the Baptist. Yeshua turned just as he reached the baptist, saw his mother. Heidi and I are standing next to her; he turned back to John and got lowered into the water.

Moments later, Yeshua made his way slowly out of the water, and got to the bank where we were.

"Woman," Yeshua said to his mother, "how did you get here?" And to us, he asked, "Who are you?"

I said, "We are from the year 2050, just travellers to the past."

"Truly, you're near to the next age."

Heidi said, "What do you mean by the next age?"

Yeshua said, "Every age is made up of 2160 years. This one that you've come to will be finishing soon. How did you travel here?"

"In our world, we have many scientists, all with their different theories about the world and the energy that it uses. We use light to travel," I said.

"My mother told me a story when I was around 12 or 13 that some people from another place had taken her along with them. So you are the ones who did that?"

Heidi told Yeshua, "We already know about you, how your life is going to end. You'll be killed by the Romans to whom the Jews gave you over."

"That's interesting! I know too, all that is going to take place," Yeshua said.

With no one else to baptize, John the Baptist came out of the water and up to where we were. Mary introduced us to him. She said, "These are the two people who came and took me back with them."

The baptist wanted to know how we did that. We told him that it all had to do with the powers of God. He seemed pleased to hear that. We listened while the baptist told us how his mother had hidden him away from those who were seeking his life. He had stayed in the wilderness for quite a long time.

Yeshua, after being baptized by John the Baptist, left and went away on his own to the wilderness.

Having stayed for a long time, he came back to the area where John was busy baptizing. We had already taken Mary back to Nazareth, and had come back again when news arrived that Yeshua had come back from the wilderness. Mary, in the meantime had shown us around the village, and had spoken to many people.

Back at the Jordan, we were surprised to see so many people listening to the preaching of John the Baptist.

John said to the people, while Yeshua was there, "This is the one that was before me. He is the *Chosen One*."

Andrew and another disciple went straight over to Yeshua, and later, Peter came. Yeshua didn't stay with the Baptist very long. Along the way, he picked up more followers, and they started baptizing the people. Heidi and I stayed around for a while, then we took Mary back to Nazareth. But before that, we met up with Philip and Nathanael. Yeshua and his disciples went to Galilee. We would meet up with them at the wedding in Cana.

We found out that we had arrived at Nazareth when the Sabbatical year was taking place. No one could work the land. And that's the reason why so many people were free to travel here and there.

On Wednesday 28th April 28 A.D., the Jewish Passover Festival would take place. Tuesday 20th April was the date for the wedding in Cana. Heidi, myself, Mary and Yeshua's brothers would all go up and meet Yeshua and his disciples there.

*

We walked the six kilometers with both Heidi and Mary on the donkeys from Nazareth to Cana, looking at the beautiful countryside with its many flowers. Cana is very high up, with fantastic scenery all around. The view is spectacular. At the wedding, there were many people gathered there. One could not miss the white canopy.

Mary introduced Heidi and me to those whom she knew. All eyes were upon us for the clothes we were wearing were not the fashion of the day.

Yeshua and his disciples arrived about twenty minutes after us. Then the bride arrived in a coach; she was dressed in white and looked lovely. The groom was also dressed in a white linen garment; he had something covering his head. I found out that the men and women had to sit separately. There was quite a lot going on at this wedding. It was explained in more detail to us later by Mary. There was the betrothal, and the nuptials. The man gives to the woman a deed before two witnesses and says, "You are hereby betrothed unto me with this ring in accordance with the laws of Moses and Israel."

Then there's the veiling of the bride; the circling; breaking of glass; all done in a circle; women dancing with women; and men dancing with men; bride and groom lifted in chair, and holding a handkerchief.

The merrymaking began, and it was found out that the wine was low. Outside, just by the door, were six great stone jars. The servants told Mary about them, and she in turn told her son Yeshua. He said to her, "Woman, what is it to do with you and me? My time has not yet come."

Mary said to the servants who stood by waiting, "Do whatever he tells you to do."

Yeshua told the servants to fill up the jars with water, then they were to take some and give it to the master of the banquet. The master of the banquet tasted, and said, "My! This is fine wine. You have left the best for the last."

After the wedding was over, we all went down to Capernaum, and stayed there for a few days. Heidi and I couldn't help but observing that most of the disciples were pretty tall. We had a good listen to some things Yeshua had to say, and we told him about what was going on about him from where we came from. James was the next to Yeshua, and we also chatted with him. He was interested to know more about our travels. Joses, the young one, chatted with us as well, so did Jude and Simon. As he drank the wine diluted with water, Yeshua asked, "Did my teaching go down well?"

"There are many people who believe in your teaching, especially about the spirit and life," I said to him. "There are some though, who are still confused with some things you said."

"I spoke just like the Father taught me," Yeshua said.

"Explain the Father to us," Heidi told Yeshua.

"The Father is God. He is the Only One. Everything that He has is mine; and all that I have belongs to Him."

Heidi, looking a bit worried asked, "Were you really sent by God the Creator?"

"Truly, the One and Only God sent me. I came from him."

Heidi said to Yeshua, "You don't realize it, but in the future where we come from your teaching has caused many people to go to war. Many buildings have been built where people could worship you; and there are many sects all preaching in your name."

Yeshua turned to James and said, "Do you hear that James, even in the future my teaching is popular, and you still don't believe in me?"

James said, "Maybe it is because you're my brother, and some of your words I can't understand."

"Later, James, later, you'll understand. It will become plain to you," Yeshua said.

I said, "I've been trying very hard to understand what you mean, when you said, *'I'm in the Father, and the Father is in me'.*"

"I spoke about spiritual life. I spoke the truth. The Father is spirit, and He and I are one and the same," Yeshua said.

Heidi said, "In our four books about you, and other books, they claim that you have not committed any sin. In fact, you challenge them and asked, *'Which one of you can convict me of sin?'*"

Yeshua said, "I think that they have got that part wrong. What I said was: which one of you can prove me wrong, if I speak the truth. Some misinterpretation I think."

After spending a few days in Capernaum, we were ready to go up to Jerusalem for the Passover. It took us just about four days with Heidi and Mary riding on the donkeys, the rest of us walking.

Passover is to celebrate the time when God brought his people out of Egypt. The Passover lasts for about seven days; a traditional Passover meal, which is the Seder. Leaven things have to be taken away from the homes. The telling of the Exodus tale, reading from the Torah.

*

Nearing Jerusalem, we saw vast crowds in inns and taverns. Such crowds we had never seen before. It was surprising that there was still space between each person, and there was no problem at all. The outer courts were filled. All around the temple, the crowds gathered.

Yeshua with his five disciples went immediately where the stalls of the buyers and sellers were. He got a piece of rope that was lying there, twisted it around a few times, then went and drove people out of the temple. We could see anger in his face, while people fled away from him. The chief priests along with the leaders in a group came up to Yeshua, and wanted to know who gave him the authority to do what he had done.

We were all shocked for we never expected to see Yeshua doing such a thing. Mary could not do anything, and the disciples too stood there watching.

"Get these things out of here," Yeshua said to the people, still not answering the chief priests.

"On whose authority are you doing all this?" They asked him again.

"This is my Father's house, and it should not be made into a market for buying and selling." Yeshua told them.

"And who is your Father?"

"The same whom you call your God."

"Show us a sign!" they demanded.

"Destroy this temple, and I would definitely raise it up again in three days," Yeshua said, looking at them with piercing eyes.

One of the chief priests was dubious saying it took almost 46 years to build this temple, and he was going to raise it in three days time?

"I have power to raise up this temple if it is destroyed."

The High Priest and leaders walked away from him, and the festival carried on as usual. Yeshua showed many unusual signs, and the people believed him to be a prophet.

6.

WAITING AROUND FOR THE CRUCIFIXION

Before we returned to Nazareth, one of the leaders came and spoke with Yehsua. We were told that his name was Nicodemus. He said to Yeshua, "You are a teacher that has come from God. No one can do the signs you've done if God were not with you."

Yeshua told Nicodemus, "In order to see the kingdom of God, you must be born again."

"Born again?" Nicodemus asked. "How can someone be born again when they've grown old?"

"You cannot enter the kingdom of God, first, you have to be born of water and the spirit. Flesh gives birth to flesh, and the spirit gives birth to spirit."

"How can this be?" Nicodemus was now surprised.

"You're a teacher of Israel, and yet you do not understand these things. I am talking about earthly things, not of things in the heaven, yet you do not understand."

Yeshua went away with his disciples somewhere in Judea.

At Nazareth we sat down with Mary, and listened to more stories from her. Her parents had placed her in the temple because they had promised to do so. Mary was privileged more than some other girls to understand about God, she was taught by the priests. She told us that her name also meant Miriam, and we told her that we read about that. Mary took us over to the millstone that was there to the right of the courtyard, and began to explain to us that it was for grinding grain. In fact, she went and got all the things needed, and asked Heidi to have a go.

It wasn't easy at all for Heidi, and she admitted it. The work was hard, and she told Mary that she was impressed that a woman like her had to do all this hard work; and still kept herself looking good. I also had a go, and found that it was really hard work. Later, Mary made some bread, and we ate it with oil and herbs.

"Were you expecting Yeshua to act the way he did when we entered the temple ground?" I asked Mary.

"I thought he had gone crazy," she said. "I don't know what got over him."

"He shocked many people, for you could see on their faces, they weren't expecting him to act that way," Heidi said.

"Did he ever talk about how he felt with the Romans around?" I asked.

Mary said, "As soon as he heard about it, he started talking strangely, as if he had some plan to bring them down."

"At the weddding in Cana, he said to you *'My time has not yet come'*. Did you you understand what he meant?" Heidi asked Mary.

"I don't think I understood much of what he was saying, but it sounds to me that his *'hour'*, the time when he would be *'glorified'* was what he meant. The angel had already told me that he will be great, and that he will save his people from their sins. So the shedding of his blood could be what the angel was announcing," Mary told us.

"So you knew all along that there was something great about him?" I said. "You have already seen when we took you back with us, how great he was for the people. These people of him, they worship him very much."

*

A few weeks later, Yeshua and his disciples were in around Nazareth. News came quickly to Mary that her son was there. We all went out to see. Yeshua was there in a circle with his disciples surrounding him, and many people standing by. Someone saw us with Mary standing there, they went and informed Yeshua that his mother was here. "Who is my mother?" he said. Then pointing to the disciples, "Those who do the will of God are my mother, brothers and sisters." He then carried on teaching his disciples. We left Yeshua and his disciples and went away.

Later, he came into the courtyard, and Mary ran out to meet him. She was talking to him, but we don't know what she said. There were quite a lot of disciples with Yeshua. They came and sat down around the courtyard, and got themselves something to eat and drink. Yeshua told the other disciples about us; that we were from another place on earth, but from the future. The seven disciples who had never met us, looked at us strangely, with a worried look upon their faces.

Yeshua turned to his disciples and said, "What I'm teaching you now has already been taken up by billions of followers. They believe that I am the Messiah who is to come into the world."

Peter said, "But Rabbi! I've already declared you to be the Messiah!"

"That is not enough, Peter, the people need proof."

In A.D. 29 Herod Antipas got his hands on John the Baptist, and put him away. Herodias was glad that that took place, he had had enough of John the Baptist.

Again, we travelled up to Jerusalem with Yeshua and the rest of the family. There were confrontations with himself and the Pharisees. They said that they were not illegitimate and had only one Father who is God. Calling him a Samaritan; and even that he was demon-possessed. Yeshua shouted back that he was from God, and that God had sent him.

"You dishonour me," he told them, "and I'm not demon-possessed. If you knew me, you would know my Father also. You're from below, I am from above. You are of this world; I am not of this world. At the time you have lifted the Son of Man, then you will know that I am he, and that I do nothing on my own, but speak just what the Father has taught me. The one who sent me is with me, and has not left me alone, for I always do what pleases him.

Another time when Yeshua and his disciples came to visit Mary, Heidi and I had a real good debate with them – especially the other seven disciples. We had met them, but hadn't at that time discussed much with them.

Yeshua was making his last trip to Jerusalem, and he

knew what was going to take place. We were there and were glad to be part of what was going to happen. It was around four in the afternoon when we all arrived in the little village of Bethany. Another two hours and the Sabbath would begin. We had taken a slow walk up, riding on donkeys. Should the Sabbath have caught us on the way, we would have stopped and set up camp, but we made it. Saturday and some of Sunday we stayed around Bethany. Martha, Mary and Lazarus greeted us with fresh drinks, and with something to eat. They treated us very nicely. Martha was not as tall as Yeshua, and she carried this small clay jar under her arm. Mary was really beautiful, like one of those princesses. She seemed to us to be somewhat shy, but once you get chatting with her, the conversation flows well. Lazarus came up to Yeshua's shoulder. He wasn't that good-looking, but was talkative, and seemed to be a nice person.

Martha, Mary and Lazarus were told why Heidi and I were here, and how we had taken Mary back to where we came from. They found it all interesting, but hard to grasp. Everyone now seated, I said to Martha, "Tell me about your brother Lazarus, and how Yeshua brought him back to life."

Martha said, "Our physician found that our brother was dead, after he examined him. So there was nothing else to do but to send word out to friends and families. We sent word to Yeshua as well."

Heidi asked, "Why didn't Mary go out with you when you went to meet Yeshua?"

"She's like that," Martha said, "she waits for the teacher to call her."

"What would Yeshua have done if he was present?"

"He's no doctor, he's only a 'Teacher'," I said.

"We would not have had to bury my brother, Yeshua would have healed him. He has the power to do so."

"So then he's God!" Heidi said.

Martha said, "He's not God, but he's the 'Messiah' we were all waiting for."

Yeshua taking a drink of his diluted wine said to Martha, "You believe that I am he. You have seen more than others can see."

We discussed many more things, with Heidi and I are questioning the disciples about Yeshua, and why they had followed him. They asked us many questions too, and they were satisfied that we weren't angels from some heavenly abode.

It was now Sabbath, and we all rested listening to stories from the Old Testament that were told to us. On Sunday, we would leave for Jerusalem. It wasn't far away, and it would take us about twenty minutes to get there. Before we left, Mary anointed Yeshua's feet, and dried them with her hair. Sometimes I got the feeling that Mary and Yeshua were close, but I think I could have been wrong. Some disciples weren't pleased about the waste.

The group of us set off to make the trip to Jerusalem with Yeshua riding on a young donkey. Heidi and Mary, Yeshua's mother, decided to walk for it would be good for them seeing that it was only a few kilometers. Martha and her sister Mary rode on donkeys too. The rest of us walked, including the half-brothers of Yeshua and the disciples.

As we came near to Jerusalem, crowds and crowds of people lined the path throwing clothes down for Yeshua to ride over; others threw down palm branches. So many people followed and shouting,

"Blessed is he who comes in the name of the Lord Hosannah in the Highest."

Arriving at the temple, Yeshua was very angry. He rushed into the temple, had words with the chief priests, and came out again. Going over to the other side of the temple, he just kept on looking at it. Then he predicted that it would be destroyed.

Then the disciples started asking him many questions as to the end of the world, and what would be the sign of his coming. We didn't stay long in Jerusalem, only had time for Yeshua to send Peter and John to make preparations for the Passover. After they had done so, we went back to Bethany. Many people came by to see Lazarus. It was at this time that the chief priests, scribes and teachers of the law started making plans to get rid of Lazarus. Here at Bethany, Yeshua taught his disciples quite a lot. Heidi and I placed many questions to Yeshua which he answered, and we were satisfied.

Thursday just before 6 pm, we all settled in the upstairs room that was prepared for Yeshua and his disciples. Back where we came from 6pm on Thursday would be Thursday night. Here, in the ancient Jewish world, it is a Friday. At around 3pm, Yeshua would die on the cross; and he would be taken down before 6pm when the Sabbath would begin, making it also Saturday, and the first day of the unleavened bread festival. This always takes place on the 15th day of Nisan. Friday the 14th –

Nisan – the day when the lambs are slaughtered.

Yeshua knew that Judas one of his disciples was going to betray him for money to the chief priests, so he had made arrangements to have this meal on this Thursday evening. During the meal, Judas left and went away. At the end of the meal, after speaking to his disciples, they all left and went over to Gethsemane. Later, on Friday morning, we heard that they had arrested Yeshua, and brought him in before Annas and Caiaphas who were both priests. Annas is the father-in-law to Caiaphas. Yeshua was also taken to Pilate who sent him to Herod, and was sent back to Pilate. Pilate found nothing to charge Yeshua with. The chief priests, scribes, and teachers of the law, and the people, called for the crucifixion of Yeshua.

Mary, Yeshua's mother was distraught, but couldn't do anything. The distance Yeshua had to carry his cross wasn't that far. It was over 500 meters. And on the way he was staggering, then falling to his knees, one could see that his body was not strong. He finally made it to Golgotha where the Roman soldiers – four of them – stripped the purple robe Yeshua was wearing from him, fitted the crossbeam to the upstanding pole, and fastened him to the cross. The Roman soldiers had after they had fastened him to the cross, drawn lots for his garments. Only a few of us were allowed to be close to the cross. The rest stood at a distance looking on.

There was Yeshua's mother Mary, her sister, also called Mary, and there was Mary Magdalene whom Yeshua loved. Heidi and I stood next to Mary, Yeshua's mother. Mary, Yeshua's mother wept all the time. At around 3pm,

Yeshua gave a loud cry, and then bowed his head. The dead had to be taken down from the cross before 6pm.

*

Just before the Greeks had come and chatted with Yeshua, Heidi and I had already spoken to him about taking him back with us. In the time that Yeshua sent his disciples out two by two, he told them that he'd be back before they had gone to all the towns. We got him inside our circle, he had to bow down a bit because he was so tall – most of the disciples were tall. And then we concentrated, and were turned into light and taken away.

*

Just like his mother, when she was here, Yeshua was amazed to see all the books written about him. He took one and looked through it, but he couldn't understand it. The language was in English, and he knew nothing about that. After he had settled in, the Sunday morning services started at 10:30am. The congregation was mainly black. Yeshua was wearing modern clothing so no one could recognize him. The decoration and architecture of the church fascinated him. He had taken in quite a lot. We seated ourselves ready for the preacher to take the service. The church was packed right down to the front door. Some children were even sitting on the floor just by the steps to the altar. The preacher started:

This Jesus, Our Lord and Saviour, was crucified, died, and was raised again on the third day by God our Creator.

The congregation said: *Amen, amen, amen. Praise be to the Lord our God.*

41

Just then a big fat woman jumped up from her seat, and shouted, *"HE'S HERE! HE'S HERE!"* The preacher begged her to sit down and calm herself. He told her that Jesus was in heaven sitting at the right hand of God. Soon, he'll return, and take charge of his kingdom. The whole congregation shouted: *Praise the Lord.*

Then we took Yeshua to another church where the congregation was mixed. The white preacher started his sermon: *"To be with Christ, you have to give up all."* Yeshua couldn't believe it all. We showed him on TV; many films that had been made about him. He saw now how big he had become in the future life. We had time to show him a few more things, then we went back to his time just in time for him to meet his disciples coming back from the mission he had sent them on.

They were full of joy, for they had done great work. Just before Yeshua had sent out his disciples two by two, he had already brought back, from the dead, the widow's son at Nain. He had also brought back the daughter of the leader of the Synagogue, back to life.

Yeshua was taken down from the cross, and laid out on the ground. Joseph of Arimathea and Nicodemus came and took charge of the body. I went and gave them a hand to take the body to a near tomb.

Heidi and I told Mary, Yeshua's mother, that we would camp near the tomb until Sunday morning. We found a spot where no one could see us, and we laid low.

7.

YESHUA'S ASCENSION

Heidi and I stayed around until the day of Yeshua's ascension came around. The sky was clear and blue with patches of clouds here and there. On Sunday morning around 3.45am something strange took place. Two men dressed in white clothing came to the tomb and rolled away the stone that was against it. There was this soft humming sound, but we couldn't tell where it was coming from. The men came out of the tomb with someone between them, we guessed it must have been Yeshua, for he was the only one in the tomb. They turned to their left and went away. Later, Mary Magdalene was there looking into the empty tomb. She couldn't understand why it was empty.

Then Yeshua appeared to her, but she wasn't allowed to touch him. After she had fallen at his feet, and he had sent her away to the other disciples, Yeshua said in a soft voice, "I know that you are there, you can come from your hiding."

Heidi and I rose up from where we were, and stood in front of Yeshua. Heidi said, "We saw two angels ... well, men in white taking you away."

Yeshua said, "They were angels. I am not in an earthly form now, but in the form ready to ascend."

"Before you leave us," I said, "where *exactly* are you going?"

"Back to the Father, he was the one who sent me."

"What we don't understand is: you said that the Father is with you. How come you are going to the Father?" Heidi asked.

I said, "And as I can recall, in one of the gospels, John's gospel, I'm sure you told Philip that anyone who sees you has seen the Father. Can you explain to us more clearly what that is all about?"

"The Father is spirit, and I am in the spirit, so we are one."

"Heidi and myself travel through light, and that's what I believe you do too," I told him.

Yeshua said, "I am light, and that's how I came into the world."

"So you will be ascending in a body of light?" Heidi asked.

Yehua said, "Yes, going up to the Father who sent me."

"So you really did bring back Lazarus from the dead? Only one of the gospels reported that, while the other three do not mention it," I told Yeshua.

"The raising of Lazarus really took place," Yeshua said. "It is something that earth people will not be able to understand. Both of you travel in light, and within the light, you see light. That is something many people won't understand."

"You'll be leaving us soon," Heidi said.

"I'll be around for another 40 days, then I'm ready to ascend to the Father."

"You said to the Jews that they are from below, and

44

you from above. Are you from another Solar System?" I enquired.

"I am on the third heaven which is the third system. The Father is greater than all."

Heidi asked, "Is Venus then, the third heaven?"

Yeshua answered, "Didn't I say that I was *'the morning star'?*"

"That's interesting," I said to him. "We on Earth know that Venus is hot, and that no life can live there."

Yeshua said, "That's where you are wrong. There's life on Venus."

Heidi said, "When we leave here we're going back to your mother, and we will tell her that we saw you."

Yeshua said, "She'll not believe you. The last time she saw me, I was hanging dead on the stake."

I said, "We'll convince her that you're alive."

Yeshua said, "I will show myself to my disciples, and not to the world."

Heidi said, "We'll stay around to see you ascend, then we'll go back to our own place."

"The Kingdom of God shall come, and I shall be taken away."

We left Yeshua, and went back to his mother. She was there with some friends. Sitting down and getting a drink, we told her that we had seen her son. She couldn't believe. "How could that be?" she asked.

We told her all that had happened after they had placed him in the tomb, and what we had seen early Sunday morning.

Heidi and I stayed around until the day of Yeshua's ascension came around.

The sky was clear and blue with patches of clouds here and there, just coming up to 10am.

The hill was in front of us, and Gethsemane not far away. We could swear that we heard a very soft humming sound, but wasn't sure what was happening. The eleven disciples were all there, plus two men in white clothing.

Yeshua was there on the top in a long white robe with widened sleeves. Suddenly, above him were white clouds. He gave commands to his disciples, and then we watched as he was taken up into the cloud.

The two men in white spoke to the disciples. We all left the hill knowing that what we had seen had actually taken place. How do we explain such a thing? We bid the disciples farewell; we had already told Mary that after the ascension, she wouldn't see us anymore.

Heidi and I held hands ... and we were gone.

THE END

BREATH OF LIFE

This poem took me about a minute to write. It just came into my head.

Breathing the breath of life
We live from day to day.
Through trouble and strife,
We've got lots to say.

Like thank you "Great One"
For a journey that we started.
We know it isn't done
'till we're parted–
From that heavy material frame,
When the solar wind shall take us speedily
To that place without a name
Then we shall feed on the spirit, but not greedily.
But we first have to endure
The harsh environmental ways
We have to live, love, hate, and even more,
While we get pounded with those fiery rays.

NATURE'S WILL

This poem just came to me so I jotted it down quickly.

I looked out and saw the sea billowing,
Great waves a-coming.
Fishes came up upon the sandy shore,
An easy catch right up to the fisherman's door.

I looked out and saw the darkened sky,
Rain falling from on high.
The day suddenly turned to night,
The thick dark area without any light.

I closed the window of my shack,
Clasped my hands and leaned back.
I closed my eyes, and kept still,
It all happened through Nature's will.

Then came the day of the burning sun,
What a ghastly heat.
It was really no fun,
Looking at red-burned feet.

It is Nature's will,
It is Nature's force.
It is Nature that can kill,
On its terrible course.

GOD'S BREATH

I always had the feeling that there was something we could tap into when things went wrong — and that was the spirit.

How can you say that God's Spirit is evil,
That His breath is nothing but a breeze?
It is that which gives us understanding and the skill
To do things completely with ease.

It is through the soul that you'll know the spirit,
The body is just an instrument.
With all the attributes that's within it,
The Spirit is Heavenly sent.

God's breath doesn't lead to death,
It's like the wind, forever moving.
It's like a summer fete,
Pleasing and amusing.

The understanding of it leads you to see,
That when things are wrong
You can ease through them easily,
And in the end, to be brave and strong.

THE SUN

It so happen that while studying astrology, I came up with this poem.

The sun came into being to do a job,
It doesn't get paid a dime or a bob.
Still, it labours daily,
From sunrise to sunset,
It hasn't stop yet.

Just a huge ball of hot gas, spinning around
Most of it hydrogen, helium, carbon, nitrogen and oxygen.
Along the ecliptic it makes a silent sound,
It is there giving life to everything, while it's Milky Way bound.

Some of the ancients worshipped it as "God",
Not knowing that one day it would dissipate.
They called it "Lord"
As it came through the Eastern gate.

There are stories that it twice rose in the West,
And settled down to set in the East.
They think it disappears, then manifest,
As a wild angry and hungry beast.

But little did they know,
That its turning and its glow,
Wasn't all for show;
It was to sustain everything below.

BIRTH OF EARTH

Just a quick poem

From the Milky Way
I observed the Nebular cloud.

It lay
There, like a shroud.

Then an object came by
And sucked the gases out.

I don't know why,
But a crushing atmospheric pressure came about.
A massive gas giant is now there
Pressure builds up.
In and around and every where.

Now the fusion reaction cannot stop.
Atoms of hydrogen dancing around
Joining together without a sound.
Producing what we call helium,
Energy that's more awesome.

Then the whole thing starts a-spinning,
Gravitation takes hold.
Then all the particles starts mingling
Now the mass starts to unfold.

My future home planet is forming,
It's hot and it's storming
Through space at a tremendous speed;
Locked around the central mass, indeed.

JUSTICE AND PEACE

I do not know what is happening, but the poems keep coming through.

Dish it out on my plate – justice.
It's not too late – give me justice.
I will wait – for justice.
I will not hesitate – I need justice.

The world needs justice,
We don't need malice.
The world needs peace,
Let the fighting cease.

The world need to rest,
Giving love, giving its best.
The world need to open its eyes
And look up to those stars in the skies.

The world has had enough,
Time to turn the page.
To one that is not so rough,
Releasing us from the cage.

When that day comes around,
There'll be laughter and a beautiful sound.
Love will be there,easily found,
When we're all space-bound.

THE FUTURE

I believe that the future can be told, but it is rather difficult.

The future will come,
No matter what anyone say.
It will change the present for some,
Giving them a brand new day.

You only have to wait,
And it will come for sure.
It will never be late,
It will knock on your door.

Even if you're not there,
It will still show its face.
It will come and share,
What it has for the human race.

The future can be told,
But it would scare the daylights out of some.
You have to take a good hold,
Being wise, and not dumb.

In cycles, they'd tumble through
Those planets high up there,
Showing a future message for you,
It could be positive or negative, I swear.

EMBRACE LIFE

I believe that we should not give in when things goes wrong.

Embrace life,
Give it a good hug.
Through troubles and strife,
Even when it's a tug.

Steady your feet with every step,
Make sure you know what you're doing.
Like on holidays, you need a good rep,
So that you know where you're going.

You may cry, laugh, weep or sigh,
Tomorrow is still drawing near.
You can be low or high,
You should have nothing to fear.

Embrace life,
Don't turn your back.
Whether husband or wife,
You have to follow life's track.

AN ATTEMPT TO MAKE MAN

This poem is strange. I don't know how it came about.

Every day
I mixed the clay;
And bake it in the sun.
When that was done,
I shaped it like a man.
I attempted to make it come alive,
It stayed there lifeless;
And you only have to guess,
I've been there from 8 to 5.

"Wake up," I cried.

Still, I wasn't satisfied.
I shouted till my throat was sore;
And to tell you more,
I almost died.

There has to be another remedy,
I took the baked dust into the lab,
So heavy it was, I placed it on a slab.
Smooth and cold, I was told,
Was part of the mystery.

I softened it up, added milk,
A bit of grass, some fine silk.
Churned it round and round,
Then I heard a strange sound,

"I, I, I, I, I."

I quickly cast it to set,
A few minutes later, I get
The feeling, I wanted to fly.
It was a foolish experiment,
So don't you ever try.

WAKE UP, BE ALIVE

Yes, I'm filled with lots of poems about space.

Way up, high up,
Is a shining star.
It is your cosmic cup,
It is your heavenly jar.

Tune in to it,
And get to know
Every single bit,
Of what to do and where to go.

It will be too late,
If you ignore good counsel.
Make a date,
And receive your starry bundel –

Of the beginning, of the end;
Of the in between;
Of your love and friend;
And of every dream.

You're of a star
Shining your light.
On earth and afar,
Every day and every night.

Wake up and see,
You are you, and not me.
Wake up, open your eyes,
Be alive, for nothing dies.

THE FIRST CREATOR

I always believe that there is a creator. This poem is just strange.

The group of viper-headed men kept on spitting,
I said: "For God's sake, open the door, and let me in."

Their breath was like a burning flame,
Their leader was one that was lame.

I went through the door, and they followed,
Such ugly faces, I had never seen.

Their clothing looked as if they were borrowed,
Their skins were pale green.

"You're surely not from this planet," I said.
"You're so thin, you look like you're half-dead."

"Come, I'll take you to see my queen,
She's kind, full of love, and serene."

"Go on, tell me, you're the creators of this mess,
I'll laugh out loud, and I'll make a guess.

You tried to copy the first creator, and it went wrong,
You belittle the weak, and praise the strong.

So it were you who founded the earth,
When it was completely covered in darkness.
The mass of water covered the dirt,
You have surely made a great mess.

The first Creator, I will praise,
All the earth belongs to him.
He set the firmament ablaze,
Now we sing songs to him.

CREATION OF MAN AND WOMAN

The idea for this poem came from the Old Testament.

A lump of clay, lifeless,
Waiting for God's breath.
Naked, without any dress,
When woken, will face death.

Joined as man and woman,
Into one flesh.
They will be both human,
Like a complicted mesh.

Joined to the rib,
They must be parted.
With the help of a gib
To complete what God started.

Now they're two,
Man and wife.
It is true,
That there'll be trouble and strife.

The two will populate the earth,
From just a single sperm.
Their children will go forth,
Spreading love, hate, and germ.

POSITIVE AND NEGATIVE

If a person act in a negative way, we look at him strangely. If he does something positively, we are pleased, But positive and negative cannot be parted.

I saw Mr Positive walking down the road,
I saw Mr Negative behind, carrying a heavy load.
They both were unable to speak,
Because their bodies were rather weak.

You cannot have one without the other,
If you do, you'll get some bother.
They both work together,
In any sort of weather.

If the place is dark,
All we need is to throw a switch.
You'll hit the mark,
When positive and negative has no twitch.

Both must be connected,
They cannot be thrown away, or rejected.
The negative will play its part,
Just like the positive from the start.

Positive and negative walk hand in hand,
In all what we do, they'll make their stand.
So don't think positive is good, and negative not,
They both work when it's cold, and when it's hot.

What about positive thinking?
And of course, negative winking?
Again, it's positive linking,
Along with negative drinking.

But no matter what you try to say,
Both positive and negative win the day.
At the very start of creation,
They came into being, through every nation.

GOD'S POWER

I know what it means to obey those who are in authority, even when they use their powers wrongly. This poem is about the "Great One".

You're mistrusting, you depend on your own power,
You don't trust in God and his strong tower.
You'll definitely be repaid,
Just like the Lord God said.

"This earth is mine," saith the Lord.
There's no other rock besides me.
I am Him, I am your God,
I will feed and protect you constantly.

I show myself to those I love,
I speak to them when they're asleep.
I send down power and love,
Like deers, I make them to leap.

I'm not a man,
And I don't change my mind.
I'll do all that I can,
To get you to the front, and not leave you behind.

A HUMAN BEING

Just sending them as they come in.
I see a human being in my land,
And I know he has the same rights as me.
Whether rich or poor, I give a hand,
I pour out love continuously.

What more can I do,
But to be myself.
To help when I can, and be true,
Give them something from my shelf.

They must try and help themselves as well,
Taking it easy as they stride,
Getting themselves out the clutches of hell,
Finding a place where love abide.

I see a human being, poor, miserable,
I understand why it is so.
I'll help if I'm able,
For life is strange, you know.

MOSES

The idea for this poem came from the bible - of course!

The king of Egypt was really afraid,
He gave the order to kill the Hebrew male children.
Through the flags, the soldiers wade,
They saved the daughters, women and men.

Moses laid in the bitumen pitch basket,
Too young to know his fate.
Jochebed had to hide him and get
Back home before it became too late.

Miriam stayed and waited,
For the king's daughter to arrive.
She didn't hesitated,
She had to save Moses – keep him alive.

The Princess knew it was a Hebrew child,
It laid there so beautiful and mild.
She held it up, then hugged it,
It was so young and fit.

The Princess was barren, Moses became her son,
When her father dies, Moses will be the next one.

Back in the palace jealousy broke out,
The king's court made comment, didn't know what
they were talking about.

The astrologers saw Moses as a threat,
He would bring Egypt to ruin.
They urged the king to put Moses to death,
Before the end of June.

As a young man Moses saw two Hebrews fighting,
Kicking, pulling and biting.
He said: "That's not good what you do,
You should be brothers and be true."

They said: "Why do you make such a big fuss?
Who made you judge over us?"

Then Moses killed the Egyptian,
And fled to Midian.

There at the well, at midday,
He sat down for a rest.
Before he had time to pray,
Maidens and shepherds put him to the test.

The shepherds were rough and tough,
Moses, much more powerful.
Their speech were bad enough,
Still they rushed at Moses like a mad bull.

The shepherds were defeated,
They can go home and tell,
How they lied and cheated,
The seven maidens at the well.

Jethro invited Moses to dine,
For rescuing his girls, Moses did fine.
Moses married Zipporah,
Jethro's daughter.

Standing at the burning bush,
An angel of light appeared.
Aaron and Miriam reminded Moses of Cush,
And the city he had spared.

After 80 years he returned to Goshen,
Everything a little more peaceful then.
He confronted the king,
With plagues and signs and everything.

"You will be like 'God' to the king," God had said.
"Aaron will be your prophet.
I'll be inside your head.
Get the Israelites out, don't be the king's pet."

At the Red Sea, the rain belted down,
The Egyptians were in sight.
The Israelites cursed and frowned
The two armies didn't clash that night.

Early morning, a fire above,
Moses with his rod, parted the sea.
The Israelites went on dry land, as light as a dove,
They were rescued mysteriously.

The waters came back and caught Pharaoh's army,
Trying to imitate the Israelites.
They failed to catch their enemy,
The Israelites watched, and stood up for their rights.

At Mount Sinai,
God landed as a devouring fire.
On a mountain high,
He communicated without a wire.

Moses let the people out to meet God,
On the very third day.
They all gathered to hear THE LORD,
His voice out of fire, it was awesome they say.

THE GIRL FROM UKRAINE

Charles, my mate wants to get himself an overseas girlfriend. I prefer to go for the British one. We both love our football club so much that we want our girlfriends to be part of it.

Getting beaten by Barnsley, Nottingham Forest caused me a lot of pain. Still, I'll get over it.'

Charles said: "Of course, you'll get over it. It's one of those things. Did you enjoy the football, though."

"Yes. One of those things , you say? I'm a loyal football fan, and I expect to see my club do well."

"Come on, they're now third in the league, and that's not bad!"

"It's awful, they should be on top." I told Charles. "I want to see them back in their rightful place."

My name is John Carwet. My friend's name is Charles Wentling. We just came out from the Barnsley ground. We went there to watch Nottingham Forest, our darling football club. They got beaten 2-1 and it left me deeply hurt.

Charles tried his best to calm me down, but he knew what sort of person I was when it came to football. Both of us were great fans of Forest, and we wanted to see the club do well.

At my flat, Charles went immediately on the computer. I went and got the teas ready. When I came back with the teas, I saw that Charles was into one of those dating sites.

"What are you looking at?" I asked him. "For God's sake don't tell me you're interested in one of them."

He was on the dating site for women from Ukraine.

"These women are *beautiful*," he told me. "Look at this one. Ain't she something?"

"I can go down to the local pub, and pick something more beautiful."

"No, you can't! Admit that you're now seeing beauty like you've never seen it before."

I said: "Almost every one of them got their lips painted with thick paint, don't like it."

Charles laughed. "That's not paint, it's lipstick!"

"It looks like paint to me. They've overdone it, too much of it."

Charles said: "What would you do if you met one of them?" He scrolled down the page, as the women appeared one after the other.

"I won't be doing anything because I'm sure I won't be meeting any of them."

"You never know," he said, still looking eagerly at the page. "I'll take this one."

I looked closer, and I had to admit that she was beautiful.

"How old is she?" I asked him.

"Twenty-two, just about the right thing. And listen to what she wrote, 'I'm an honest woman, looking for the right man. I'm family minded and I love children.'"

"Is she communist?"

"No. She isn't! You don't think I would—"

"Yes, you *would*, Charles. You'd pick up on any beautiful thing, communist or no communist."

"Ukraine has no communist party. It is not accepted there."

"We've just come out of a stadium with about 13,000 spectators, why didn't you try and find a woman from among that lot. Why go overseas?"

Charles wasn't listening to me at all. He was already making contact, sending an email away.

"Nothing's going to come of it. She's far too young. And how are you going to meet her. Oh! No. In Ukraine?"

Charles heard me this time. He said, "You've hit it right. We shall go to Ukraine."

"It's not safe there. I'd rather stay here and cry my heart out over Forest."

Charles said: "Forest can take care of itself even if things don't go down well for a few games. Who's going to take care of you? You need a good beautiful woman as your wife."

"There are some nice beautiful British women around."

"But will they be as faithful and honest as these women here?"

Charles was trying to make a point. I said to him, "Okay! you take an Ukranian woman, I'll take a British one, is that ok?"

A couple of days later, Charles received an email that his girl was coming over for two weeks.to see if she'd like it. Well, now, we don't have to go to Ukraine, and I could look around to find me a British woman.

In town, I was coming out of one of the department stores when I saw this woman. She hopped passed me, gave me a smile, half turned back, and carried on.

This was my chance, I told myself. Don't make a fool of yourself now. You have to play your cards right. If you want her, you have to make your move.

I didn't see anything wrong at all with British women. Some of them were really beautiful and well-built. Once they get to know you, they'll stick with you through thick and thin.

The woman I had just seen was just in front of me at the cash register. I managed to talk with her just as she stepped out the door. "How'd you like to go and have a drink with me?" I said to her very confidently. "There's a bar just across the road."

"Okay!" She accepted.

We went to the bar across the road, and I ordered some wine. When we had our drinks, I said to her, "My name is John Carwet, and I'm crazy about football. What about you?"

"I'm Irene Butley," she said, "and I like football too."

"That's great," I said. "Then I could invite you to one of Forests' home games. How would you like that?"

"I will come."

We started in conversation about many other things, and I actually invited her to my flat. I wanted Charles to see what he was blind to see – a real British woman. She had it all. Her lips weren't painted red like those women Charles were after. I also liked the way she dressed, nice and neat not overdoing it.

Charles came around just in time for me to introduce Irene to him. He looked shocked. I said to him, "What is it? Is there something wrong?"

"No. No ... it's just ... that's really *strange!*"

"What is?" I wanted to know.

"The girl I'm dating on the internet, guess what? Her name is Irena."

"You're joking with me," I told him. "That's a coincidence!"

"Have you got a photo of her?" Irene asked

Charles brought a number of photos and showed them to Irene. I had already seen them. Irene questioned Charles some more. "What made you go overseas to Ukraine to find a woman? Don't you like British girls?"

"Of course I do. But there are certain things I just cant stand. British women like their alcohol. Some of them drink more than the men."

"So that's what put you off?"

"Another thing about them is, they keep on sending useless things on the phone. And if they're not happy, they'll storm at you."

"Are you listening, John?"

"Yes, I heard every word he said. But Charles is like that. It's ok with me."

"Anything else Charles that you don't like about the British women?" Irene questioned him.

"They don't often come right out and say to the man 'I love you!' they just like calling us funny names. One thing I must say, though, if you make a joke, they'll laugh their heads off." Charles was letting it all out.

Irene said: "As a woman, I have to say that these women that you're after are really pretty in the face. Is that all you're looking for?"

Charles said: "Not only are they pretty, but their

standard of living is pretty high. And they always stand behind their man."

"And then give him a push when things go wrong," Irene said.

"I think Irena would make a good wife. She's young, and I can train her into many good things."

"The first thing you have to train her to do is…" I broke in, "…is to love Forest. If she do that, then she'd be the best woman in the world."

Irene said: "Charles, you keep on mentioning the British women, but surely you must mean the *English* women. There's a difference between *English* and *British*."

"Yes, silly me," Charles replied. "There's definitely a big difference between the two."

"Coming back to the way Englsih women are," I said, "you'd better watch out if the relationship breaks up."

"Why? What happens?" Irene asked.

"They become totally out of control, and give up everything."

"That's not true, John. Not every English woman is like that, yes, there may be one or two. Most English women are strong. They don't give up easily."

"From what I know of the English women," I said, "I'm not referring to British women here, they're very reliable, falls deeply in love with one man. They goad their mates to take up something that is worthwhile."

"Irena," Charles declared, "is a very good cook at her age. She likes the beach and the park. Her family means a lot to her, and she would like to have her own family."

"That gives me an idea," I said to Charles. We could take her to Skegness if it's a nice sunny day. We could stay late till evening. I'll bring my guitar, and we could have a sing song."

"She'd like that," Charles admitted. "It would be just great. I'm also planning to go to the army surplus shop and get some equipment for two days."

"*CAMPING?*" I almost shouted. "Are you *crazy*? The girl wants luxury."

"I think it will go down well." Charles had his mind made up.

I asked Irene if she was free on the dates when we would be going up to Skegness for the day. And at another time when we would be going camping for two days. She said that those days were OK.

*

We all went up to Heathrow airport to meet Irena arriving from Ukraine. We stood there watching the people coming off the plane. I saw this young thing, gorgeous as can be, and straight away I knew she had to be Irena, Charles' flame.

When she met us we greeted each other and then we went into the car.

Back at Charle's flat, we all made ourselves comfortable while Irena and Charles hugged and kissed each other. She started telling us about the flight over, and how her parents, families and friends came to see her off at the airport.

"You're really beautiful," I said. "Charles was right. Ukrainian women are beautiful indeed, and not in the face alone, but also in the figure."

"Watch it," Charles said, funnily. "She's mine, all mine."

Irene said to Irena: "Is it really so beautiful in Ukraine, and is it peaceful there?"

Charles had the coffee ready. We each took a cup, and poured out what we needed.

Irena answered: "It's still not good between Russia and ourselves. Yes, Ukraine is still beautiful. There is still clashes in some areas. They accused our people of carrying out terrorism against them. With Russia, you don't know what they'll do next; they keep on building forces in Crimea."

"That's awful," Irene told her, "that they should be treating you like that! Anyway, enjoy your stay here."

"Thank you!" Irena said with a smile.

"See, Charles," I told him, "there's still trouble around that area. My foot is not going there. Not just now, anyway."

"It's not the whole country. Just certain parts," Charles assured me. "Let's not bother much about that. Let's get this Ukrainian lady a lively two weeks here."

Irene and myself left Charles and Irena to get on with their love life, and we went back to where Irene lived. Her flat was small but nice. Decorated well, just like I expected someone like her would have it. She set the coffee on and we had a cup.

"What a couple they are," I said to Irene. "I think that they'll fall deeply in love, and then there'll be wedding bells."

Irene said: "From what I've read about those Ukrainian women, they are very romantic; and very passionate too."

"Aren't you romantic and passionate?" I asked her.

"British women are romantic and passionate in a

different sort of way," Irene explained to me. "And they show their love very deeply, and honestly."

"Well, I'm glad I made the move first to get at you. You could have turned me down when I asked you out. Why didn't you?"

"I just had strong feelings about you, that's why."

I said: "I also felt something inside of me telling me, *Go for it*."

Irene said: "We shall see how we get on."

The trip to Skegness came on a day that was really sunny and beautiful. We left Nottingham for Lincoln then headed up to Skegness. It took us just over two hours. there were many people up there already and the place was spectacular. We went on quite a number of the rides and many other attractions. Then when evening came, we found ourselves at the water's edge just the four of us. We started chatting about quite a lot of things, and I sung a few Beatles' songs along with a few from other artists. Late at night, we drove back to Nottingham.

I could see that Irena had a good time, and Charles was pleased that it went down well.

When we got to Nottingham, getting out the car, Irena gave Charles a big kiss. She said: "That was really romantic! I enjoyed every bit of it."

Charles said, "I'm glad you liked it, it's my pleasure."

We all went up to Newcastle to watch Nottingham Forest win 2-3. They had me trembling close to the end, but they held on and came away with the points.

Without Irena knowing what was going on we went and set up camp in a farmer's field. It drizzled for an hour and then the sun was out all day. There was a stream nearby. The tent was up, camp beds all there, and the burner outside was burning away while the lunch was being prepared.

Charles brought Irena across the farmer's field. They came to where Irene and I were preparing lunch. I looked to see how Irena was taking it and was surprised to see her all chuffed. That was good, she didn't mind what we were doing. We had knocked up something special for her, and when she tasted it, she gave her compliments. She didn't say anything much against the camping. She must have done this sort of thing back in Ukraine. She told Charles that she liked hiking, taking long walks over the mountains; and walking along the beach looking at the stars.

The two days camping went down well. Everyone enjoyed themselves. It stayed sunny so we were lucky not to have any rain, except for the drizzle when we first came.

We took Irena to Nottingham castle, told her stories about Robin Hood; and took her to the Robin Hood Legacy. We visited Wollaton Hall, City of the Caves, the National Justice Museum, the Aboretum, a Victorian park with many trees. It was opened in 1852. We took her to other places over the two weeks that she stayed.

Her stay now ended, we took Irena back to Heathrow where she boarded her plane back to Ukraine.

END

Also by John Gumbs

Jehanne 978-1-78222-571-3
The Trial and Burning of Jehanne 978-1-78222-609-3
Aitch H 978-1-78222-628-4
Jay G 978-1-78222-656-7
Heidi 978-1-78222-682-6
Sheila 978-1-78222-729-8
Just Mates 978-1-78222-751-9
Jay G, Assignment to the Netherlands 978-1-78222-782-3

JEHANNE

John Gumbs

THE TRIAL AND BURNING OF
JEHANNE

John Gumbs

AITCH

Jay
G

John Gumbs

Heidi

John Gumbs

Just Mates

John Gumbs

Sheila

John Gumbs

JAY G
Assignment to
The Netherlands

JOHN GUMBS

www.ingramcontent.com/pod-product-compliance
Lightning Source LLC
Chambersburg PA
CBHW070806120626
46557CB00002B/738